THE
BACKWARD
DAY

THE BACKWARD DAY

STORY BY

RUTH KRAUSS

PICTURES BY

MARC SIMONT

THE NEW YORK REVIEW CHILDREN'S COLLECTION
New York

THIS IS A NEW YORK REVIEW BOOK
PUBLISHED BY THE NEW YORK REVIEW OF BOOKS
1755 Broadway, New York, NY 10019
www.nyrb.com

This edition published by agreement with HarperCollins Publishers

Library of Congress Cataloging-in-Publication Data

Krauss, Ruth.
The backward day / by Ruth Krauss ; pictures by Marc Simont.
p. cm. — (New York Review children's collection)
Summary: Having decided that it is backward day, a boy dresses himself first in
his coat, last in his socks, and continues in that way with the cooperation of his
family.
ISBN-13: 978-1-59017-237-7 (alk. paper)
ISBN-10: 1-59017-237-X (alk. paper)
[1. Morning—Fiction. 2. Family life—Fiction. 3. Humorous stories.]
I. Simont, Marc, ill. II. Title.
CURL PZ7.K875Bac 2007
[E]—dc22
2007006747

ISBN 978-1-59017-237-7

Cover design by Louise Fili Ltd.

Printed in United States on acid-free paper.

1 3 5 7 9 10 8 6 4 2

A little boy woke up one morning and got out of bed. He said to himself, "Today is backward day."

He put on his coat.

———

Over his coat, he put on his suit.

Over his suit, he put on his under-wear. He explained to himself, "Backward day is backward day."

He put on his shoes. Over his shoes, he put on his socks.

Then he turned his head backward as far as he could, to see over his shoulder, and he walked backward out of his room and backward down the stairs.

He walked backward into the breakfast room, backward past the place that was his place at the table, and the chair that was his chair. He walked backward until he reached his father's place. He then turned his father's chair backward to the table and sat. He tucked his father's napkin in at the back of his collar.

His father came into the breakfast room.

"Goodnight, Pa," the little boy said to him.

His father stood and looked at him. "Goodnight," he said.

His mother came into the breakfast room.
"Goodnight, Ma," the little boy said to her.
His mother stood and looked at him. "Good-
night," she said.

His baby sister came into the breakfast room.
"Goodnight, Baby," he said to her.

His baby sister stood and looked at him.
"Goodnight," she said.

Then his father went to the place that was the little boy's place at the table. He turned the little boy's chair backward to the table and sat. He tied the little boy's napkin backward around his neck.

His mother went to the place that was his baby sister's place at the table. She turned his baby sister's high-chair backward to the table and sat. She tied his baby sister's bib backward around her neck.

His baby sister went to the place that was their mother's place at the table. She pulled their mother's chair around backward to the table and sat. She pushed their mother's napkin in down the back of her dress.

The little boy looked at his father. He looked at his mother. He looked at his baby sister. He said, "I'm so full I can't eat another thing."

"Me too," his father said.

"Me too," his mother said.

"Me too," his baby sister said.

The little boy pulled out his napkin from the back of his collar. "Time to go to bed," he said and got up from the table. He turned his head backward as far as he could, to see over his shoulder, and walked backward out the breakfast room.

Backward up the stairs he went and backward into his room he went—backward oh backward oh backward oh backward oh backward
and . . .

. . . back again out of his clothes and back into bed. He yelled very loud from his bed to his father and his mother and his baby sister, "TO-DAY IS BACKWARD DAY." He yelled again explaining, "BACKWARD DAY IS BACK-WARD DAY."

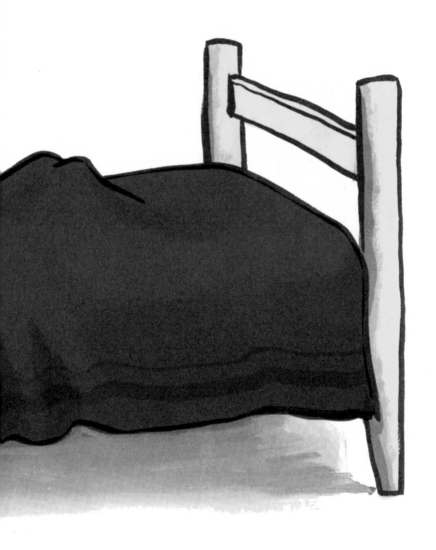

His father got up from the table.
His mother got up from the table.
His baby sister got up from the table . . .

. . . "Time to get up out of bed again," the little boy said to himself. He got out of bed again. He put on his underwear. Over his underwear, he put on his suit. He explained to himself, "When backward day is done, backward day is done." Then he put on his socks and shoes and yelled, "BACKWARD DAY IS DONE."

RUTH KRAUSS was born in Baltimore, Maryland, in 1911. She attended the Peabody Institute of Music in Baltimore and received a BA from the Parson's School of Applied Art in New York City. During the 1940s and 1950s, Krauss spent time at the Bank Street Writer's Laboratory, where authors were encouraged to work directly with children; her *A Hole Is to Dig* (published in 1952) was written collaboratively with nursery school students and was illustrated by Maurice Sendak. The many outstanding illustrators Krauss worked with in the course of her long career include her husband, Crockett Johnson, the creator of the comic strip "Barnaby" and author of *Harold and the Purple Crayon*. A playwright and poet, as well as an author for children, Krauss died in 1993 at the age of 81.

MARC SIMONT was born in Paris in 1915, the child of Catalan immigrants. He studied art with his father, a professional illustrator, and at several schools in France and America, where he moved when he was nineteen. Simont has illustrated nearly one hundred books, working with authors such as Margaret Wise Brown, James Thurber, and Marjorie Weinman Sharmat (on the *Nate the Great* series). He is also the author of several books (most recently *The Stray Dog*) and the translator of poems by García Lorca and others. Simont received the Caldecott Medal for his illustrations to *A Tree Is Nice* by Janice May Udry; *The Happy Day*, another collaboration with Ruth Krauss, is a Caldecott Honor Book. Marc Simont lives in West Cornwall, Connecticut.